EDGAR
ESCAPES!

EDGAR ESCAPES!

Edgar J. Hyde

CCP

© 1998 Children's Choice Publications Ltd

Text supplied by Alan J. Henderson

ISBN 1-902012-14-3

Printed and bound in the UK

Contents

Chapter 1

This is my tale and I shall tell it to you. I am Edgar J. Hyde, the teller of dark tales from beyond the grave. I was a scholar and a tutor long, long ago. Dear reader, I will reveal the person behind the stories, where I am from, and the purpose I have.

Now, I ask you to read on – if you dare!

*　　*　　*

After bringing many other ghostly and despicable tales to your notice I decided that I must tell my own story. I am sure you, my readers and faithful fans, are more than a little interested to know who the man, Edgar J. Hyde was and what he is today. Confronted with this demand for knowledge, I felt it was only correct that I should submit my story to you. Dear reader, I would not be anything without your attention.

Producing my tales in written form was not an easy task for one such as myself who reaches you from beyond the grave. Today you have powerful computers, e-mail, modems and the Internet, but these are of little assistance to me. I must confess I do not understand how these machines operate. That is for you and your kind to learn about. Instead, this tale comes to you through the work of my most devoted servant and scribe, Hugo.

The night was long and dark for Hugo when I came to him, filled with evil and menacing thoughts. It was as if it was destined for our minds to meet. If I had not appeared in his thoughts I think he would most certainly have gone mad and killed himself that very night. Hugo was very close to the edge.

I entered Hugo's thoughts as he momentarily dozed. My aim was to get him to tell my tale. He, thankfully, accepted my request and wrote down everything that I told him from beyond the grave. This book was published under my name and not his. Nobody would believe that a man such as Hugo could come up with such a story; be it fact or fiction. Although he had written books, he had never written one like this.

Hugo heard my voice and faithfully wrote all I said down on paper. For this work alone, I thank him with all my soul.

At first Hugo was not sure what to make of me and what I was telling him. He thought it was just another indication that he was losing his mind. People had told him, or he had heard somewhere, that hearing voices in your head was a sure sign of mental illness. For a moment he despaired that it had come to this. Did it all have to end in madness, he thought?

Then, quite suddenly, he began to listen more sharply and believe what I was saying from the spirit world. All thoughts of madness had disappeared from his mind. He began to realise he was experiencing something special – something only a very few people will ever understand.

Our thoughts seemed to meet and we understood each other fully. I wanted Hugo to write down my tale, and he wanted to hear what I had to tell. In many ways, for each of us, it was perfect timing.

How fortunate I was to come across Hugo on that night. Here was a man that would

Chapter 1

listen without having to question what I would tell him. His was an agile brain that had been lying dormant through years of self-doubt and self-pity. I turned the key and unlocked the power of his mind to the task of hearing my story and getting it published. How lucky I was.

Hugo was not a handsome man. The loss of his hair, at an early age, served only to exaggerate his large nose and ears. He was also a tall man and that meant most people who met him were uneasy and frightened of him. It had always been a cause of concern and frustration to him that people, who did not know him, thought he was a menacing character.

A talent that Hugo possessed, but nobody appreciated, was for writing. He had penned a few novels and sent them off to publishers. The only replies he ever received from them were rejection notes. This had dented

Hugo's confidence about his ability to write and made him very depressed. He had taken a number of part-time jobs to make ends meet, but these only depressed him more.

I had a tale to tell and Hugo proved to be a very good listener and writer. That night when I entered his thoughts he was in the depths of despair. He was close to the edge of insanity and could well have decided it was time to end his life. Thankfully, he listened to me and I listened to him. He told me of his problems and worries and I, in turn, told him of mine.

It seemed to lift a burden from his shoulders as he told me of his life. I was eager to listen and allow Hugo to become calm and confident in my presence. Soon, we reached a point where we trusted each other.

From my prison in the spirit world, I had found a living ally on the Earth. I was so pleased.

Chapter 1

    In the darkness of a stormy night he began to write my story for me.

Chapter 2

My tale begins many centuries ago in the Middle Ages. I was born on a stormy All Hallows Eve (now known as Hallowe'en) in the year of Our Lord 1396. My father, Joshua, was a teacher in the household of the powerful Baron de Rochelle. My mother, Eve, was delighted, or so I am reliably informed, to see the birth of her only child. They decided to call me Edgar Joshua, and thus I was christened so.

My earliest memories are of being frightened of the dark in the draughty rooms of the Baron's Castle where we lived. I remember sitting, frozen by the fear of what was out there in the darkness. The Baron's hounds would howl, and cast iron gates leading to dungeons would crash shut in the middle of the night. Sometimes even horrific screams of pain could be heard from those poor fellows that found themselves in the Baron de Rochelle's dungeons. He was famed throughout the land for his terrible torture of prisoners. It was reckoned that once a man went into the Baron's dungeons he would never be seen alive again.

We lived in the Baron's huge castle because my father was a tutor to his sons. Father instructed them mainly in French, Latin, Mathematics, History and the Bible. In these olden times only the offspring of wealthy people such as the Baron received any education. The rest of the population, Monks apart, could hardly read and write. Luckily, being the son of a tutor, I was afforded the luxury of an education.

I can always remember my father saying, "It is education that sets us apart son."

By this he meant that we were very fortunate to be educated and, thus, respected because of it.

Even the Baron himself, Guy de Rochelle, with all his wealth and power had a grudging admiration for my father and his learning. The Baron knew that without an education his sons would ruin all the work he had put into his castle and lands.

Father was a strict but fair man. You knew where you stood with him. The Baron's boys knew that too. If they did not pay attention then my father would come down hard on them. He would thump their heads together or wrap their knuckles with a stick. There was no use in them complaining to their father. He believed in strong discipline and whenever his sons complained about their treatment at the hands of my father, he would make sure their punishment was doubled.

My childhood appeared quite ordinary to me, as I did not, in my early years, appreciate the benefits that an education affords. I managed to avoid the plague, small pox and any other number of the fatal diseases that were very common back in those days. War and famine were also real threats in my early years. Scarcely a year went by without a poor harvest or the castle coming under attack from the Baron's enemies. The Grim Reaper took many boys and girls, whom I knew and had played with. Death was constantly around us and threatened to strike at any time.

As I grew out of my infancy, other boys of my age were set to work in the fields and got by on their wits and brawn. They would be expected to become soldiers, herdsmen and servants. I was a very studious child and had no time for their rough play. In time, I began to spend less and less time in their company and more in the footsteps of my father and other adults.

I fact, I began to dislike other children because of their lack of education and manners. I loathed their stupid games and silly giggling. They could be so cruel and unkind to each other for no reason at all. Children were just so annoying to me that I longed to grow up quickly and escape from them completely.

But, I found myself in a strange position. It was taken for granted that I would follow in my father's footsteps and also become a tutor. You cannot be a tutor without children to teach. But, if it was only one or two of the foul little creatures, I could probably stand it, I thought. If I persevered I was sure I could put up with a few wretched children.

I had no other ideas about what I wanted to be and just accepted that the path towards becoming a tutor was my destiny. I suppose I could have worked in the royal household or the government of the land, drawing up treaties or writing down new laws that were made. My father assured me that people who could read and write were always in demand. However, I took the easy path and just modelled myself on my father. I think he was pleased that I chose to follow him into being a tutor.

The years passed and my education grew. I became fluent in both Latin and French to the extent that sometimes father and me would not speak to each other in English for days at a time. It was our little game. Although this led to some people viewing us with suspicion, as if they thought we were foreign spies plotting the downfall of the land.

I knew that I could not be a student of my father forever. Having passed my 18th birthday it was time for me to find a position as a tutor away from my family and the safety of the Baron's castle. It was time for me to enter the adult world and earn a living for myself.

Father said, "It's time for you to set out on your own, Edgar."

I gulped with trepidation at the future that lay before me. My father had said he would speak to Baron de Rochelle about the possibility of me taking up a position in one of the castles of his friends and allies. Now, very quickly, everything was about to fall into place. I was on my way.

"If I'm not ready now, then I never will be," I replied to father.

Father then said, "The Baron awaits you."

I nodded and set off towards the great hall where the Baron could be found. Approaching the great hall, the door lay ajar. A great fire was roaring in the hearth, and warming his hands at it was the huge figure of Guy de Rochelle, the Baron.

I gave a feeble cough at the entrance to attract his attention. In all my years in the castle I had never had the occasion to speak to him directly. I wondered if he even knew who I was?

The baron did not even turn to see who it was and boomed, "Come forth Edgar!"

I walked briskly towards him at the fireplace and spoke, "You wished to see me, Baron de Rochelle?"

"Indeed I do," answered the Baron as he turned to face me.

The Baron scratched at his massive black beard for a few moments, looking me up and down while he did so.

"You're a bit of a skinny young lad," he remarked seriously.

That observation made me really nervous and my knees began to tremble.

He snorted and said, "Your father says he has taught you well and you are now ready to take a position as a tutor."

"That is what I intend to be," I replied trying to sound as calm and collected as possible.

"Good," pronounced the Baron and slapped his massive hand between my shoulder blades.

The effect of this was to send a dull thud right through me and send me flying forwards. Baron de Rochelle sneered for a moment at my lack of strength. He did not really like scholars, such as myself, but he knew that education was a powerful tool to have in your armoury.

He continued, "Your father is a wise and

learned man and has taught my sons well. As a reward I have found you a position with Baron de Montford to teach his sons. They are some twenty leagues from here."

"That is very gracious of you Baron," I said and smiled.

"Do you know of the Baron and his Castle?" he inquired of me.

I replied, "Yes Baron, I shall look forward to taking up my position."

"You can make your way there from tomorrow and present yourself to Baron de Montford in three days time," concluded the Baron.

Baron de Rochelle then waved me away and said, "I have more pressing matters to attend to now, Edgar."

I bowed and said, "Thank you, Baron."

As I walked towards the door the Baron cried, "I hope you turn out to be as good a tutor as your father!"

I was thinking along these same lines myself as I pondered my future employment in the castle of Baron de Montford. But, there it was. My fate had been decided for me. A tutor I was trained to be, and a tutor I was going to be!

The very same evening I gathered together some of my belongings in a bundle for the journey to Baron de Montford's castle. I didn't really enjoy my farewell supper with my parents, as I was too nervous about the trip that lay before me.

"Twenty leagues are a very long way to travel, Edgar. Are you sure you will be all right?" asked my concerned mother.

Before I could answer her, Father said, "He'll be fine – it's a great opportunity for him."

"But what is that Baron de Montford like? Will he treat Edgar well?" Mother asked him.

My father looked a bit stumped at these questions.

"I've never seen him, but if Baron de Rochelle recommended Edgar, then I can't see any problems," he said.

The fact that nobody knew anything about Baron de Montford and his ways made me nervous and I hardly said a word for the rest of the evening.

"You'll come back and see us soon, Edgar, won't you?" Mother said.

"Of course I will," I replied, "when the Baron lets me."

Chapter 3

I awoke at dawn the following day to a fine spring morning. The birds were singing sweetly and the mist was just beginning to lift off the fields surrounding the castle. This was a good day to start a new life. After a large bowl of thin gruel and some bread I mounted my donkey and waved farewell to my parents.

"Have no fear, son. You will do well – I'm sure of that," Father said.

It reassured me that at least my father had

no doubts about my ability. Unlike myself!

"Take care now!" cried Mother as I left the castle courtyard and went through the castle gate and across the drawbridge.

I clutched at my dagger as she said this to me. There were indeed a lot of nasty things that could happen to me on the way to my new employer. Twenty leagues (60 miles in today's terms), was a huge distance back in those olden days. The journey on my donkey would take at least three or four days. I viewed this as a lot of time to be on my own and open to attack.

Apart from the vagabonds that roamed the country just looking for people such as myself to rob, there was the threat of wild animals too. In these olden days packs of wolves were still at large and, when hungry enough, it was said they preferred the sweetness of human flesh. Huge bears with dribbling jaws and razor sharp claws roamed in the woods. You might even stumble upon a wild boar, which would charge – and that would be the end of you!

The first day of the journey was the worst. My route was through a great forest where I had to reach an Inn before nightfall. I jumped out of my skin at every noise that came from the trees. Fear made me think that there were thousands of eyes belonging to beasts and robbers peering at me, just waiting for the right moment to pounce upon me.

Then, up ahead I suddenly heard voices. It was a knight on horseback followed by his servant on foot. My heart was pounding as we came to meet each other on the path.

"Who might you be then, boy?" The knight said.

"I'm Edgar Hyde," I replied in my deepest voice to sound as unafraid as possible.

"Never heard of you. Where are you

heading?" he questioned me.

"To the castle of Baron de Montford. I'm to be the new tutor," I answered.

"Ah, de Montford. I know him well," he said and paused for a moment. "Good luck to you!" he added with a laugh.

They passed by me and left me wondering why the knight had made that remark and laughed. Was there something I should know about Baron de Montford or his children?

When the light began to fade at the end of the day I was heartened by the smell of wood smoke and meat being cooked. The Inn I was to stay at that night was close by.

The stout owner welcomed me in and said, "We've the best meat and the finest ale in these parts, young man."

Over supper I explained to the owner that I was to be the new tutor at Baron be Montford's castle.

Chapter 3

His eyebrows raised when I mentioned the name.

"Is there something about the Baron I should know?" I asked.

"Only rumours. Nothing to worry your young head about," said the owner.

It was late and I retired to my bed. For a while I was restless as my thoughts turned to what the owner had meant by "rumours". Then I fell into a deep sleep.

I waved farewell to the owner and set out on the second leg of my journey. Once again the path was mainly through the shadows of a thick forest. Less fearful now of the surroundings, I was looking forward to my day's travel. In the back of my mind, though, I knew that there was no Inn where I could stay this night. I would have to spend all the hours of darkness in the open. It was something I had never done before.

The day passed pleasantly enough, with

almost nobody on the path to cause me any concern. It was only as night began to fall that I began to feel ill at ease. What would the darkness hold for me tonight? Every flutter of wings or rustle of the wind in the branches drew my instant attention. I was a nervous wreck.

I hastily made a fire and sat hunched around it. After plucking a chicken that I'd bought from the innkeeper I roasted it over the fire. It smelt delicious as the fat oozed out and basted the skin. The thought of food managed to calm me down.

As I was about to eat I noticed that my donkey was becoming very restless. His ears were pricked upright and he was scraping the ground with one of his front hoofs. Could there be something out there? Had the smell of the food attracted an unwelcome visitor?

Then it happened.

Chapter 3

A terrible and spine-chilling, hungry howl came from a nearby wolf! I froze with fear. Then there was a moment of silence and I breathed out with relief.

The wolf howled again. This time it sounded louder and closer. I stood up and grabbed my dagger in one hand and a flaming stick from the fire in the other.

Could there be more than one wolf, I thought? Maybe there was a whole pack of them waiting to tear me to pieces. My mind raced with visions of huge horrible fangs dripping with blood, their mad eyes staring at me with murderous intent, faces distorted and made ugly with snarls, baying for my flesh.

As I peered into the darkness with the aid of the flaming stick, I thought I saw movement. Suddenly, the light caught a pair of eyes. I gasped with fear. Would it charge and attack me?

In an instant the wolf was gone again. The fire must have frightened it off. I never heard him howl again that night, although I remained awake for most of it waiting for the worst to happen.

Eventually, I could remain awake no longer and fell into a deep sleep. I awoke with a startle in the warmth of the morning. My fire was out, but I reckoned a wolf would not try to attack a man during the hours of daylight. I was a very relieved young man that morning.

After gathering my things I set off again on the trail to the Castle of Baron de Montford. I would be glad when I reached my destination. The perils of life outside a secure castle were not for me.

Chapter 4

On the afternoon of my third day's travel I came to the head of a valley and there spied a castle in the distance before me. It was the castle of Baron de Montford. A shiver suddenly ran down my spine as though someone had walked over my grave. Was it an omen for my fate at the hands of the Baron?

As I approached the castle it seemed to loom out of its surroundings with a dark and ominous feel to it. I saw that the drawbridge was lowered and approached the guards at the portcullis.

Looking above the portcullis as I neared, my stomach turned at the sight of two rotting heads impaled on spikes above the entrance to the castle. A crow swooped down and landed on one of them. It began to pick at what remained of the face.

"What be your business young lad?" A guard said.

I was stunned by the horrible sight above me and did not reply.

The guard gruffly said, "Are you deaf, young man? What be your business at the castle of Baron de Montford?"

I introduced myself with, "I'm Edgar Hyde, new tutor to the Baron's children."

The guards peered at me, and seeing no threat, raised the portcullis to allow me to enter the castle.

"Come with me," ordered one of the guards.

I dismounted my donkey and led it across

a busy castle courtyard. A few pigs and hens scattered out of our way. People at work in the courtyard stared suspiciously at me and murmured comments to each other as I passed by.

"Leave the donkey there," the guard said, as he pointed at a post.

I tied the donkey to it and was then led up some steps and into a hallway. The guard rapped at a huge oak door with the bottom of his sword and pushed it open. My mouth was completely dry with the anticipation of meeting the Baron.

In a flash there was a yelp of laughter and two boys came rushing out of the doorway and knocked me to the ground. For a second I sat there on the floor shocked and stunned. The guard then offered me his hand and pulled me up.

With a grin on his face, he whispered, "That's what you've got to teach my lad!"

"What's that commotion?" cried a deep voice from the gloom of the large room.

"It's a boy who claims to be your new tutor, Sire," the guard answered.

"Ah," said the voice, "you'd better show him in."

We walked across the room to a figure hunched over a table covered with important looking scrolls.

"So you are Edgar Hyde?" said the man behind the table.

"Yes," I replied, "son of Joshua Hyde, tutor to Baron Rochelle."

The figure rose from behind the table and said, "I'm Baron de Montford."

He was another giant of a man with a mane of jet-black hair and a long scar running down his left cheek. There was then a pause, which seemed to last for an age as he looked me up and down.

The Baron broke the silence and said,

"You've already met my boys – they knocked you to the floor there."

"No harm done," I replied trying desperately to win favour with the Baron.

Putting his huge arm around my shoulders the Baron walked me across the room to a window overlooking a courtyard. His boys were playing down below us.

"My boys need educated, Edgar," he said.

"Indeed Baron," I replied.

"As you can see, they are high-spirited lads, but they need some of their rough edges taken off," he continued.

I nodded in agreement whilst wondering what I had let myself in for.

The Baron then shouted through the window.

"Boys, come up and meet your new tutor."

A few seconds later there was a clatter of footsteps as the boys flew into the room.

They looked wild and ragged with dirty faces, which I thought was not fitting for the sons of a Baron.

"Let me introduce Edgar Hyde," he said to his boys.

The boys looked at each other and giggled.

"This is Richard," said the Baron pointing to the taller of the boys, "and this is Thomas."

I could tell straight away that the boys were putting on an act of shyness and innocence in front of their father. Richard had a mop of fair hair, while Thomas had brown hair. They were both now staring at me, trying to size me up.

"Pleased to meet you!" I cried, "I shall look forward to teaching you both."

Richard then said to his father, the Baron, "I hope he lasts longer than the last one!"

Thomas then kicked his brother on the

shin and the pair of them flew out of the room again with shouts and screams.

The Baron laughed and said, "Lovely boys!"

I was glad he thought so, because on first impressions I did not like the look of them at all.

Following our introductions, a fair young maid was summoned and she led me to my quarters. She brought some bread, cheese and ale for me to lunch upon.

"Is everything alright for you, sir?" the maid asked.

"Fine," I replied, "but please call me Edgar, you don't have to be so formal with me."

She blushed with embarrassment and bowed her head. Servants were not supposed to be on first name terms with educated people such as me. But I had taken a liking to her and was in need of friendship in my new surroundings.

"What's your name?" I asked her.

She smiled and replied, "Gertrude."

As she was about to leave the room I questioned her.

"Well Gertrude, can you tell me what happened to the last tutor?"

By her expression I seemed to have put her on the spot, but she replied:

"He was here one day and vanished the next."

Chapter 5

At the time I didn't pay any heed to what Gertrude, the maid, had said. Tutors often come and go, so why had I any reason to be suspicious? I had only just arrived at the castle and been introduced to a couple of tearaways who were to be my pupils. Had I really expected anything else?

That very afternoon I was introduced to the Barons chief counsellor. He was a short, stout man by the name of Godfrey. My first impression of him, with his darting eyes and restless posture, was that he was a man always on the look out. He knew what was going on around the Baron and knew how to look after himself. He was a schemer.

"Come and I'll show you around," said Godfrey.

We walked along the ramparts and discussed the Baron and his lands.

We looked out on to the rolling green hills that stretched for miles.

"Is all this the Baron's?" I asked.

"Oh yes! All that and beyond the horizon too!" cried Godfrey. "He's one of the wealthiest men in the land."

Godfrey showed me the grain store, the water well, the animal pens, the guardroom and, most disagreeably, the dungeons.

The smell of death and despair was all around as he showed me where the unfortunate guests of the Baron were kept. As we stood above the entrance to a dungeon I could hear moans from a poor wretched soul inside.

"Water! Water!" said the voice from the darkness.

I felt such pity for the pathetic voice. In sympathy, I said to Godfrey:

"Shall I give him some water?"

"Certainly not," Godfrey sniffed at my request, "or the Baron will have you down there with him."

"Oh, I see," I said and gulped at the thought of ending up in a horrible dank dungeon dying of thirst and hunger.

"Didn't you see the poor wretches above the portcullis on the way in?" Godfrey added.

I nodded as the image of the rotting heads flitted through my mind again.

"The Baron is not a man to be questioned or doubted. You have already seen what happens to those who dare to do that," Godfrey continued.

My blood ran cold at the thought of what I had let myself in for by coming here to become the Baron's tutor. Still, Godfrey had given me fair warning about the Baron and it was up to me not to make him angry. Godfrey obviously knew how to manage the Baron and I supposed I would have to learn how to handle him too.

Godfrey and I had dinner together that evening. I hoped to pick up some more tips on how to handle the Baron and keep on his good side. We gorged ourselves on a delicious roast suckling pig and some ale. Gertrude helped to serve the meal and we smiled coyly at each other.

Godfrey noticed us exchanging a smile.

"Ah, I see you've made a friend already," he said with a sly look.

I looked sheepishly at the floor and

Godfrey laughed so much that he choked on a piece of food. This made me begin to laugh and we both chortled away for a few minutes. At last, I began to feel relaxed. Filled with food I lay back in my chair and scratched my full belly.

Godfrey grinned.

"See! There are advantages to working for one of the richest men in the land," he laughed.

I laughed and nodded in agreement.

It was getting late and as it had been a long and exciting day for me I felt quite tired. Retiring to my quarters I felt quite drowsy. I was just about to slip off into sleep when I heard a rustle in my room. Was it rats? Or had a thief come to steal what little I had? Maybe it was a madman intent on killing me to satisfy his blood lust? My heart raced with fear. My dagger lay on the floor on the other side of the room. I was defenceless in the darkness of my room.

"Shh, Edgar, don't make a sound," a female voice whispered.

Then out of the darkness I could make out the face of Gertrude with a shawl wrapped around her head. She came and sat close to me.

She whispered, "I'll get flogged if they find me here so keep your voice down."

"What are you doing here?" I questioned her as quietly as I could.

"I've come to warn you," she said.

"Warn me?" I questioned her in reply.

"Yes, it's about the Baron's boys," she heeded me. "Be very careful of them. They could lead you to your downfall."

Smiling I joked, "I can handle a couple of ignorant boys – it's the Baron I'm worried about."

"So you should be," said the maid, " but cross the boys and you cross the Baron!"

Chapter 5

In a flash I realised what must have happened to the previous tutor, and possibly all the tutors before him too. They probably upset the boys in some way and word got back to their father with severe action being taken. Severe in this place almost certainly meant deadly.

We both jumped as we heard distant voices.

"I must go now," said Gertrude fearfully.

"Thank you for warning me," I said as she departed silently into the darkness.

I lay there all night deep in thought about how I would handle the situation. What had I let myself in for by coming here?

Chapter 6

The next few days came as a complete shock to me. Never before had I came across two such horrible and troublesome boys. I had little time for spoiled children and their ways, but they were unbelievable. They were completely indulged by their father, and because of his position of power nobody ever dared to complain about the behaviour of his boys.

Richard and Thomas had received a limited education but that seemed only to cover the areas of lying, cheating, stealing and insolence. The boys were expert in all these fields – there was no more I could possibly teach them.

I remember one afternoon I summoned them to a lesson. They dragged their heels and had grim faces as they entered the room. Guessing what had happened to the previous tutors I felt somewhat nervous as to how to approach them and win over their attention.

"Right boys!" I said, "I know we've got off on the wrong foot but I'm paid to teach you and that is what I'm going to do."

Richard immediately produced a gigantic yawn to indicate that he didn't care what I did or said.

Something snapped. It was one lazy yawn too far for this tutor. He had to be put in his place!

Looking towards Thomas I said, "You don't want to end up an ignorant oaf like your brother do you?"

Richard looked amazed that I had dared to make such a comment. What had I done?

An evil smile came over Thomas' face.

"I'll tell my father what you just said about my brother."

Disappointed by my failure to get through to them I raised my voice.

"Don't you want to learn?" I pleaded.

"One day I'll be Baron, and all this will be mine," Richard answered.

"Yes, and I'll help him rule these lands," added Thomas.

I tried to reason with them.

"But you won't be able to rule properly without an education."

The boys scoffed at my comment and made faces at me. With that they turned and skipped out of the room laughing.

I shouted after them in despair.

"Your father will hear about this!"

What was I to do? If I didn't follow

through my threat to report them to their father the boys would have even less respect for me. But if I tried to tell the Baron his sons were such horrors how would he react to the news? Would he fly into a rage and draw his sword to run me through with it?

I never expected things to turn out like this. Should I resign my position or just run away? It began to make sense to me now why the boys' last tutor had mysteriously disappeared.

I needed to think things through. As it was a fine afternoon I decided to go for a ride in the forest and do my thinking there. Looking at my donkey tied up in the courtyard, I decided that riding out of the castle on it would do little for my self-respect either. So, I approached the Captain of the guards to see if I could use one of their horses for the afternoon.

"Something wrong with your donkey?" asked the Captain.

"I just want to go for a good old gallop that's all," I replied.

"Fine," said the captain and shrugged his shoulders, "you can have that big mare on the left."

He led me over to the horse.

"Are you sure you can handle one of these?" he enquired.

"Of course I can," I answered hastily, although my experience of riding was not that great.

I patted the beast on the side of the neck and marvelled at its strength. It would do me good to get away from the castle for a while, I thought.

Bending down and forming a support with his hands the Captain said, "Up we go then!"

Suddenly there I was off the ground

astride a massive horse. I began to feel better already.

"Watch her, Edgar," said the Captain, "she can be a bit flighty that one!"

The horse yielded to my orders from reigns, heels and voice. There we stood, positioned in the middle of the courtyard ready to go for a ride in the forest. Then from behind I heard those familiar evil giggles from Richard and Thomas. I turned around to see Richard with a big wooden stave in his hands. He came rushing towards my horse with the stave raised.

"No, Richard!" I screamed.

It was too late. Richard smacked the poor horse solidly on the right hindquarter. It reacted instantly and reared up on its hind legs with a frightened neigh. I grabbed the reigns tight to try and regain control. The horse then bucked around the courtyard a few times and I felt the battle to keep control was lost.

It all seemed to happen in slow motion. I parted company with the horse found my-self flying upwards into the air. On reaching the top of my upward path I saw the laughing faces of Richard and Thomas pointing at me. I also caught sight of Gertrude holding her hands to her face in anguish. Then I fell towards the ground suddenly realising that my head was about to crash onto a flagstone.

Landing on the stone with a deadly thud I can remember nothing apart from the sight of the children laughing at my fate and Godfrey rushing them away from the scene of their crime.

I awoke about a day later lying in a bed. My arms and legs wouldn't move. I knew then that I was about to die. My hearing and sight were fading, but I still had the power of speech. There seemed to be many people in the room but suddenly I became aware of the giggling presence of Richard and Thomas. My blood boiled with rage. Other children were eagerly trying to enter the room to goggle at a dying man. How typical of kids, I thought.

"You boys!" I groaned, "see what you've done to me?"

My head filled with black, evil thoughts as I looked up the foul, hideous boys who had brought me to this position. Me, Edgar J. Hyde, what had I done to deserve such an untimely ending to my life?

It was then that I decided to hatch a terrible curse upon the boys, and thinking about it further, a curse on all children forever more! I always had loathed children and now was my last chance to place a curse upon them all.

"You boys! You children!" I screamed, "I will have my revenge on you all! You have cost me my life and now I swear I shall ruin yours. I place a curse on you all so that evil and fear will haunt you at every turn. Every night I will come into your thoughts and into your dreams. I'll come back to haunt you all and drive you mad!"

The exertion of making my curse had made me very weary, and I drifted into a sleep not knowing if I would ever wake up again.

My eyes then flickered open. Before me stood an old man with a long white beard dressed in a purple cape with weird symbols on it. What a strange sight! Was I seeing things?

"Edgar, you are much troubled, but please lift the curse you placed," said the old man.

I was angered by the old man's request.

"Who are you to make such a demand of a dying man?" I demanded.

"I'm Edwin," he said.

Still filled with anger I stormed, "How do you intend to make me lift my curse on children?"

"You are a learned man, Edgar," he replied, "I too have learned much in my many years. But my knowledge is ancient and mystical. I know of the earth and its natural powers – of life and death, love and hate, revenge and forgiveness."

"Get to the point old man," I croaked.

"I'm what some call a sorcerer," said Edwin.

A sorcerer? I had heard of them of course – but I'd never spoken to a man who claimed to be one.

"The Baron heard of your curse and sent for me," he continued. "Either you remove the curse or I'll cast a spell on you which will banish your soul to an eternity of imprisonment on this earth."

Unimpressed I mocked Edwin.

Chapter 6

"Do your worst, old man, I'm about to die anyway. I curse all your children! A sorcerer indeed, hah!"

Edwin sighed and peered deeply into my eyes. He then struck his long metal staff on the stone floor, which produced an unnatural ringing that filled the room.

"I, Edwin the sorcerer, do cast a spell upon you, Edgar Joshua Hyde. May your curse be worthless as long as children have good thoughts in their minds. Your soul shall remain here on earth, alone, in limbo, whilst the power of my spell lasts."

He then sprinkled a potion over my body and I felt a sudden chill come over me. I drew my last breath and my life ended on May 1st 1414.

I was dead!

Chapter 7

Being dead is no fun. That may seem obvious to you, readers, but I can assure it's true. What's even worse is being under a spell that prevents you from seeking the revenge that every ounce of your being aches for. Edwin's spell had condemned my soul to an endless wandering on this earth. I was trapped. Neither in heaven nor hell – I was stuck in between.

Can you imagine what that is like? Every day is the same. I existed in the spirit world, but I could have no influence on the world of the living from which I was so cruelly snatched by those despicable children. How badly I wished I could escape the spirit world and come back to life to have my revenge on Richard, Thomas and all the other hideous children that lived in the world.

Godfrey and Baron de Montford decided to dispose of my body in the river nearby. They did not want to draw attention to what the boys had done and decided to cover up the whole incident. It was as if I had never even been to the Castle of Baron de Montford.

My body was taken by some guards and dropped, unceremoniously, into the river. I looked on from the spirit world as my young innocent body floated down the river and began to rot. My parents would never know what had become of me, and each went to their graves heartbroken at my disappearance.

I watched from my soul prison as Richard and Thomas grew from horrible boys into horrible men. They never did receive a proper education and even managed to dispose of a few more tutors over the years. I felt sorrow for those poor unfortunate men, like me, who had set off with such high hopes only to be crushed by the evil that existed in the thoughts and deeds of two little boys.

Though they were only young men, Richard and Thomas were green with envy for their father's position of power. One fateful winter night they took matters into their own hands.

Baron de Montford sat alone at his great table reading some documents by candlelight. His sons entered the room quietly with murderous intent.

"Ah, my boys," said the Baron warmly.

The sons looked at each other not knowing what to say.

"What can I do for you this dark night?" their father inquired.

"I've come to claim what's rightfully mine!" Richard cried.

In a flash, swords were drawn and blows reigned down upon their father. They hacked and stabbed at the defenceless Baron until he was still.

With his last breath the Baron could only whisper.

"Why? Why?"

With their devious plan in mind, the sons then shouted.

"Murder! Murder! Someone has killed the Baron! Close the gate! Lift the drawbridge! Find him! Find him!"

The castle guards came rushing in to find the dead Baron. In a state of panic and confusion they believed the story of Richard and Thomas, that an intruder had murdered their father. Amidst the chaos they set about searching the castle for the fictitious assassin.

Richard knew that recently a new stable lad had been employed at the castle. He headed, with some guards, straight for the lad's sleeping chamber.

Bursting into the room he cried:

"There he is! He must be the murderer!"

The startled lad could offer no defence as the guards first beat him and then dragged him off to the dungeons to be put in chains. They tortured the poor boy with hot irons to try to make him confess to the crime, but he would not.

Godfrey knew there was something strange about the murder of the Baron. Why would a simple stable lad want to murder the Baron? But, as always, Godfrey was thinking of his own position and dared not question the story told by Richard and Thomas.

The following day he was hanged without a trial, despite pleading his innocence. It was a gruesome death as he hung there for hours slowly having the life throttled out of him.

Richard stood there with a feint smile on his face as the execution proceeded. Behind him Thomas looked on with more jealous and black thoughts in his head. He now wanted the power that his older brother had inherited.

Thomas didn't have to wait long to seize his chance. A dispute arose between rival Barons that eventually led to them waging war with each other. Thomas decided to make his move.

The battle took place on a gloomy day in driving rain. The rival forces clashed in a forest clearing. As the fighting progressed, both Richard and Thomas dismounted their horses to enter the thick of the fray. All the time, whilst watching for his own safety, Thomas kept a sharp eye on where his brother was.

Richard became separated from his guards and was pursued into the forest by two men. Thomas followed behind them hoping to see his brother slain. Instead, Richard turned and with sweeping blows cut both his attackers down, although taking a heavy blow to his sword arm.

Recognising his brother, Thomas, approaching he smiled.

"See! The day shall be ours!" he cried.

Thomas came nearer and replied:

"The day shall be mine!"

Instantly, he plunged his sword through the heart of his brother.

As he smiled with the thought of having killed his brother, and thereby opened the way to him becoming Baron, it was suddenly all over for Thomas too. A crossbow bolt flew into his head and he died instantly.

Good riddance to them both! They got what they deserved, but how dearly I would have liked to have dealt their fate to them myself.

As for Edwin, the sorcerer who consigned my soul to endless wondering, he just disappeared one day. Nobody knew where he went or why. It was as if he had vanished into thin air.

Chapter 8

It gladdened my soul to see the terrible demise of the boys who had caused me an untimely death. Still, however, I longed to be brought back into the world of the living to wreak my revenge on all the horrible children on the Earth. The problem was to somehow overcome Edwin's spell. I had to get children to stop thinking good thoughts and then, one day, I might be able to return from the grave into the land of the living.

It didn't take many years before an idea came to me. If only there was some way to get the evil thoughts contained in ghostly horror stories into every child's head. I would then stand a chance of overcoming the power of Edwin's spell. What I needed to do was to find a method to saturate the minds of children with nasty ideas. It was simple. Books!

At the start of the 15th century, when I died, horror stories were told by word of mouth and this was how they passed from generation to generation. The fairy stories you may have heard were much more gruesome and frightening back in my time also. Sadly, through the passage of time, they have become very watered-down affairs and hardly frighten anybody at all now.

Another way that people were told of devilish deeds and ghostly haunting was through plays. The most famous writer of plays was a man called William Shakespeare. He began his work in the 16th century and wrote great plays such as Hamlet, Macbeth and Othello. Some of these plays had dark themes of ghosts, murder, jealousy and revenge.

As I explained earlier, very few people were educated enough to read. Hardly any books existed at the start of the 15th century at all, and they were mainly the Bible. Every book was ornately written by hand – and that took ages! Wouldn't it be wonderful if there was a way of producing millions of books with evil stories in them for children to read? Then their minds could become full of evil thoughts and Edwin's spell would be broken. I would be free.

People in China had been printing with individual wooden blocks for centuries, but this was a very slow method. What I needed was for somebody to discover a way to produce books quickly. As I roamed the spirit world, it was in 1450 I came across some interesting events going on in Germany. I eavesdropped on a conversation between Johann Gutenberg and Johann Fust in the town of Mainz.

Gutenberg said to Fust, "What do you think of this?"

He showed him a page printed using individual letters, which he called type, set in rows to form words and sentences. Gutenberg's method meant that each page of a book could be composed and printed quickly. Many copies of a book could also be produced. It was so much faster than writing by hand.

"How did you make this?" said Fust, "It doesn't look like it has been written by hand."

Gutenberg replied, "It wasn't, it was made by a process I call printing."

He then pointed to the huge wooden printing press that he had made himself.

Fust looked at it and said, "That's incredible!"

This was exactly what I needed – a way of producing lots of books easily!

Johann Gutenberg explained what printing was to his companion and the possibilities it had for making money from producing books for people to read. I willed with all my might that Fust would agree to lend Gutenberg some money to work further on the new process called "printing". Luckily, he did so. The first printed bible was produced in 1455.

To my amazement and joy, printing spread all over Europe. A man called William Caxton brought it to London around 1470. He managed to produce 100 books in his working lifetime. This may seem a very small amount, but to me, it was an incredible start. The ball was rolling and I could feel things were turning my way.

The production of more books had meant that many people could be educated and would be able to read. They could then pass on their reading skills to others. I longed for the day when there would be millions of books and millions of readers. Maybe then enough children's heads would be filled with enough devilish thoughts to allow me to escape my soul prison and come back to life.

Edwin's spell upon me depended on children having good thoughts in their heads. I intended one day to change all that and escape. I would come back to life and have my revenge on all the children of the Earth.

It took a few centuries, but printing became faster and faster. The introduction of steam power and keyboards to make the type in the 19th century allowed many copies of many different books to be produced. Now what I needed was for people to come up with ghostly horror stories for people to read.

A young lady came to my attention in 1818. Although she was only 21, Mary Shelley wrote one of the most chilling novels ever. It was called *Frankenstein*. The story was about a brilliant Genevan doctor, called Victor Frankenstein, who becomes obsessed with bringing the dead back to life. He achieves this, but immediately sees the possibility of taking this further and creating a new, incredibly powerful being. He manages to bring life to a gigantic creature that he has assembled from bodies stolen from their fresh graves. Instead of making an improvement on the human form, the creature he gives life to is unspeakably repulsive and horrific to behold. The real horror is that the creature is tormented with misery and disgust at its own being. The creature is filled with hatred for its creator because he has rejected his creation and has a terrible lust for revenge. Unlike the monster you may have seen in the old movies, Mary Shelley's monster was capable of feelings and emotions and had a longing for affection that its creator made impossible because of its disgusting appearance – this was the real horror of the story of Frankenstein. The creature seeks to destroy everything that the doctor loves and ultimately brings about Frankenstein's own downfall. With more stories like that one I thought I could stand a good chance of coming back to life myself!

I also heard of a young man in the United States of America struggling to be a successful writer. His name was Edgar Allan Poe. I looked over his shoulder as he wrote a ghostly tale called *The Fall of the House of Usher*. It was as if I had told him to write it myself. A horrible tale about ghosts and madness set in an old house. He also wrote other frightening tales including *The Murders in the Rue Morgue* about a madman murdering people in Paris. Great stuff!

At the end of the 19th century one of the most famous horror tales of all was written. I felt a great sense of anticipation as Bram Stoker wrote *Dracula*. Here was a tale that millions would later read and recoil at. It was based on the legends from Transylvania about blood sucking vampires that would come in the night and draw the very life from you! Tales like these helped to make me, Edgar J. Hyde, a very happy soul down through the years.

So, as we approached the 20th century, loads of ghastly tales were being written and read. What I needed now was for children to start reading them. Concerned parents were afraid that ghostly tales would warp their little darlings' brains. What did they know? That's exactly what I wanted. That was my key to freedom and revenge!

Chapter 9

As we approached the millennium I could feel that my day was coming soon. I had waited over 500 years for the chance to be brought back to life. They were long and lonely years with only my hatred of ghastly children and that fool, Edwin the sorcerer, to keep me company on my endless wondering on this Earth.

Much to my joy, children were reading more and more ghastly horror stories. Horrible tales were told in comics, cartoons and the even in the games that children played.

As their minds were filled with these devil-ish stories I could feel the power of Edwin's spell starting to fade.

Of all the children on the Earth, I stumbled upon two in particular that offered me great hope in my quest to regain life and have my revenge. Bobby and Ruth Harrison were their names. They appeared just like normal children, with normal parents, living in a normal house and in a normal town. What made them special to me was that they were absolutely crazy about anything to do with ghosts, horror and the macabre. It was their obsession.

Bobby was thirteen – two years older than his sister. They were very similar in size and both had shoulder length black hair and thick black-rimmed glasses. Ruth and Bobby were very close to each other and united by their love of gore and horror. Other kids in the neighbourhood thought they were weird and avoided them, but Ruth and Bobby didn't care. As long as there was something spooky to be read or watched they were happy.

Bobby and Ruth spent all their time reading terrible tales, watching ghostly movies, or playing frightening games with each other. Their bedroom walls were completely covered with posters and pictures of fiendish characters from the stories and movies they had seen. In keeping with their fascination for all things evil, they always dressed in black.

Despite my hatred for children in general, I found this pair to my liking because of the possibilities they offered me. I saw in them my chance to be free again. Their minds were just so full of dark and horrible thoughts. They were a joy to watch from my home in the spirit world.

One night Bobby burst into his sister's room.

"I've got the new book by Dr Death!" he cried as he waved the book aloft.

"What's it called?" questioned Ruth while jumping from her seat with excitement.

"*Evil in the Crypt*," Bobby said with glee.

"Oooo, sounds great," said Ruth. "Do you think it will be as good as *The Dungeon of Terror*?"

Nodding his head Bobby answered, "Yes, of course – Dr Death has a real talent for horror."

"His last one was so good, I couldn't think of anything else for weeks!" said Ruth.

With a wicked grin Bobby pulled another copy of the book from under his black jumper.

"I knew you couldn't wait to read it, so I bought you a copy as well."

Ruth, jumping with joy, was delighted with the surprise.

"Oh thank you Bobby, we can both read it together now!" she gushed.

"Yes, that'll be fantastic!" said Bobby.

"Why not start right away?" Ruth cried.

"Why not?" replied Bobby.

Having agreed to read the horrific book by Dr Death together, Bobby sat on the bed next to Ruth. She put on the bedside lamp, which had a black shade and a green bulb. The effect was to give the room an eerie green glow. The pair of them loved the sort of atmosphere that it gave to the room.

Ruth offered Bobby a jelly baby, which he accepted with a knowing smile. The pair of them then gleefully bit the head off the baby figures in a ritual they both enjoyed. It was one of their odd little evil games.

Eagerly they began to read. Both concentrated entirely on the text without any wandering of their attention, apart from the odd smirk which fleetingly appeared upon their faces when something gruesome happened in the story. The only sound to be heard was the biting and chewing of jelly babies.

As they became more engrossed in the evil nature of the book I could sense that the day would soon be mine. I could feel that I was becoming stronger as their heads filled completely with dark and horrible thoughts. Edwin's spell was beginning to weaken. They read on some more, and I suddenly felt that it was my time. Their heads were completely full of dark and evil thoughts.

Summoning up all my power I willed myself back into the land of the living. In an instant I was alive again, standing in Ruth's bedroom. I was flesh and blood once more.

I gasped as air entered my lungs for the first time in 500 years. Blood was coursing through my veins, and my heart was beating like a drum inside me. There, all at once, were all the sights, smells and sounds that I had craved for centuries. It felt great to be alive again!

Stretching out my hands and then clenching them again to feel the power in my muscles I could hardly believe it. I had come back from the dead. I had escaped!

My appearance in Ruth's bedroom had not attracted their attention, though, as they were concentrating so much on the book. This displeased me and reminded me of why I hated kids and wanted my revenge upon every last one of them. There I stood, breathing again after 500 years and they didn't even notice me! What a cheek!

"Don't mind me," I said.

They both jolted and looked up instantly. For a time their jaws dropped and they were speechless.

"Let me introduce myself. I'm Edgar J. Hyde," I told them.

Bobby ventured to speak with a tremble

in his voice.

"How did you get in? What do you want?"

"Oh, I just want some of your time and some of your ideas, that's all," I replied.

Ruth, stared sternly at me and quizzed me.

"Why are you dressed like that?"

"Like what?" I said.

It was only then that I realised I was wearing 15th century clothes in 1998. There I was standing wearing a smock, leggings and a hood. I didn't realise that when I returned to the living world, it would be in the in which clothes I had died. They must have thought I was on my way to a fancy dress party.

"Let me explain . . ."

Chapter 10

The fear brought on by my appearance out of nowhere began to disappear and Ruth and Bobby sat silently, and listened with great interest, as I began to tell them my tale. I told them of how I died at the hands of those horrible boys, Richard and Thomas. However, I did not tell them about my hatred of all children and how I dearly wanted my revenge on all of them. Nor did I tell them about my attempted curse and the meddling interference from Edwin the sorcerer.

I kept these details from them because I wanted to use their love of horror to hatch my plan to have my revenge on all the children of the earth.

My plan was a simple one. I would fill the kids heads with such vile and spooky stories that, quite simply, they would all be driven mad! The combined dark and evil thoughts of the children who read the books would grow and grow, until children everywhere were driven insane by the sheer weight of nastiness inside their heads.

After telling them of my death, Ruth sympathised.

"What a terrible way to die – you had so much of your life to live."

"Yes, very sad," I replied. "But now, thanks to you, I'm able to live and breathe again."

"But how did we help you to come back from the dead?" inquired Bobby.

I lied to them and said, "It was only through your dedication to learning and reading, and your great concentration that I managed to come back."

Ruth cried, "Really?"

Wiping away a fake tear from the corner of my eye, I said, "Yes my dear children – you have saved me from an eternity of meaningless wandering."

That fooled them. They swallowed my story hook, line and sinker.

I then explained to them, "We have much to do."

"We?" said Bobby.

"Yes, my dear friends," I said, "I have many tales to tell from my centuries in the darkness beyond the grave."

"Do you mean you want to write and publish ghost stories and alike?" Bobby asked me.

"Bobby, that is why I chose to come to

you and Ruth," I said to them. "You are so intelligent, so thoughtful and so understanding."

It was so funny to see them believe every word I said to them. They really thought they were going to do themselves a favour by helping me. How little did they know! My revenge was going to be so sweet!

"I want children everywhere to read my stories and enjoy them in the same way that you two enjoy a good ghost story," I continued.

"What can we do to help you?" said Ruth.

"Well, you can copy down what I say and maybe put it onto that computer of yours," I replied.

Bobby jumped in, "That's a great idea! We can then send them off to a publisher and get them printed."

"We'll be rich in no time at all," cried Ruth.

Money! I hadn't thought about that. How could I forget the lure that money had? When your soul has been in limbo for 500 years you lose any idea of the value of money. Of course money was important in the 15th century too, but very few of us had any at all in those olden times.

Still, I allowed myself a grin at the thought of Ruth and Bobby thinking they would make themselves rich and happy by helping me to publish my devilish tales. My intention was to use them, and then drive them insane!

I must admit that Ruth and Bobby were very good to me; the little fools. They gave me money to find some lodgings and gave me some of their father's old clothes so that I would not stand out in the crowd. Most of all, they gave me their time and attention to allow me to tell them some of my evil tales. How they loved every minute of it!

Over the next few weeks we managed to produce the drafts of six books. I sent extracts off to a publisher and almost immediately he replied asking to see more. A meeting with a Mr Tolstoy of Globalmania Books was arranged. I could tell from his letter that he was desperate to do business with me.

Globalmania was one of the biggest children's publishers in the world. They had offices everywhere and their books were sold in all the shops. If I could persuade them that my books were a winner, then I'd be well on the way to having my revenge.

"Come in Mr Hyde," said Mr Tolstoy.

I walked into his plush office and sat in a comfortable chair.

Mr Tolstoy spoke rapidly.

"This stuff is dynamite!"

"I know," I replied with an air of confidence.

Chapter 10

"It'll sell like hot cakes all over the world!" Tolstoy added.

I gave him a broad smile.

"I do hope so," I said.

"If you sign this contract now, I can get the books into production straight away," said the enthusiastic Mr Tolstoy. "They'll be in the shops all over the world in a few weeks' time."

"Where do I sign?" I asked.

Tolstoy looked at me strangely.

"Don't you want to read the contract? Aren't you interested in how much you are going to make out of this deal?"

"I'm sure I'll make plenty of money, Mr Tolstoy. Just show me where to sign," I replied.

Tolstoy leapt from his chair and said, "Fabulous! Just sign right on the dotted line there," as he pointed to the bottom of the contract. He couldn't believe his luck that I had been so easy to deal with.

After signing, Tolstoy slapped me on the back and cried, "I'm—we're going to make a fortune out of this!"

I smiled again and said, "I hope they have the desired effect."

Chapter 11

The weeks up until the books being launched seemed to last like an eternity. Now, I had been in limbo for around 500 years, so I knew a thing or two about waiting. But, every minute of every day seemed to last forever. I just couldn't wait to have my revenge.

Ruth and Bobby were also irritating the life out of me. They were so keen and happy they just made me sick. On many occasions I wanted to tell them what I really thought of them and that they were doomed. Alas, I had to wait a while yet.

I called Tolstoy on the telephone to see how the books were progressing. He was still filled with great enthusiasm for the project. This gladdened my impatient heart.

"We're set for a world-wide launch on October 31st," he said.

I laughed at the timing and said, "How good of you to launch the books on Hallowe'en."

Tolstoy continued, "The launch will take place in London, New York, Paris, Sidney, Hong Kong, Tokyo, Johannesburg and everywhere else you care to mention."

"Sounds like we'll have lots of readers then," I added.

"You bet!" cried Tolstoy, "We've got TV advertising, billboards, competitions and free gifts all lined up for the launch."

I was humbled by the effort being put into making these books. Everybody was so eager and enthusiastic it sometimes made me weep. They had no idea at all what my goal was. If I had wanted fame and fortune I could have written books on history, as I had seen so much of it down through the centuries –but I wanted revenge.

All I had to do was wait for Hallowe'en and it would all fall into place. Kids, all over the world would be driven mad by my evil little books. I could hardly wait!

The days dragged by until it reached October 30th. Only one day to go and then I would unleash havoc upon the minds of children across the world. What could possibly go wrong with my plan?

That morning I received a message from Mr Tolstoy to come into the office to arrange some last minute details about the launch. I thought nothing of his request as a book launch the size of this one was bound to have the odd hitch here and there. Of course I wanted everything to run as smoothly as possible, but I accepted that problems might occur.

"Just to sort out some interviews and stuff," said Mr Tolstoy.

"Would you mind if I brought my two little companions, Ruth and Bobby," I asked him, "they have been such a help?"

"No problem, Mr Hyde, bring them along," he replied.

That afternoon we set off in a taxi to the Globalmania Books offices. Bobby and Ruth were very excited about going to meet such an important and powerful man as Mr Tolstoy. I was excited too, but for my own personal reasons of revenge. The hour was getting nearer.

As we entered the Globalmania building, Bobby and Ruth were awe struck by the enormous size of the place. The foyer was floored and walled in marble and huge leather seats were placed everywhere. It was like a jungle with all of the tropical plants and the odd fountain here and there.

"Gosh, it's huge," said Ruth.

"Yes, they are one of the biggest publishers in the world," I told them.

"Will our books be sold everywhere, Edgar?" asked Ruth.

"I certainly hope so," I replied with a grin. "In fact, I hope that every child in the world gets to read one soon."

We were shown through the building and up to Mr Tolstoy's office.

Tolstoy greeted us with a huge smile and said, "How are you Edgar? And you two must be Ruth and Bobby. Come on in and have a seat."

Anxious to know how the launch was progressing I quickly asked Tolstoy, "Is everything on schedule then?"

"Yes, of course – no problems, just relax Edgar," he said confidently.

I explained to Tolstoy, "Bobby and Ruth have been a great help to me. I couldn't have done it without them."

The children beamed with pride at my comments. What idiots that they really were.

Walking over to a TV, Tolstoy picked up a video and said, "Here's the advert that's going out tomorrow all over the world."

Putting the video in the machine he said, "You'll love this!"

The screen was blank for a few seconds as the tape advanced to the start of the advert. We looked on eagerly with anticipation.

Then to my utter dismay an old familiar face appeared on the screen. I recognised those old wrinkles and the long white hair and beard.

"Oh no! Please no! It's that old fool Edwin!" I screamed.

Every part of my being turned cold at the sight of the old sorcerer. What did he think he was doing?

"This isn't right!" cried Tolstoy.

Ruth and Bobby laughed for a moment at the confusion and then quickly shut up as they looked at my terror stricken face.

I turned on them and screamed.

"Shut up you stupid horrible kids – I hate you all!"

Tolstoy looked shocked by my outburst.

"Calm down Edgar, this is no way to behave."

"Oh, you shut up too! You pompous idiot!"

My blood ran cold as I heard Edwin's old voice. It reminded me of the time when he put the spell on me all those centuries ago. How could this be?

"Edgar, you shall not have your way," Edwin said.

"I will! I will!" I raged at the image of Edwin on the screen.

A clearly frightened Tolstoy asked me, "Do you know this man on the screen?"

"Of course I do. It's Edwin the sorcerer – from the 15th century," I cried in response.

Tolstoy raised his eyebrows.

"Are you feeling alright, Edgar?"

"No, not any more!" I cried as I could feel that my plans were about to go up in smoke.

Edwin's old voice continued.

"Edgar, you shall not have your way."

Filled with anger I screamed at Tolstoy.

"Turn it off – I can't stand it!"

"No leave it on, Mr Tolstoy!" cried Bobby and Ruth together.

I lunged at the video recorder but Tolstoy grabbed me and pushed me back.

"Really, Mr Hyde!" he said in disgust at my behaviour.

Now I was in a state of blind panic at the

thought of my plans being thwarted by the sickeningly good Edwin. I picked up a heavy ashtray and hurled it at the TV screen. The screen blew outwards toward us in thousands of little pieces.

Tolstoy reached for a telephone.

"Get security up here right away! This Edgar J. Hyde character has gone mad. He's dangerous!"

Then to my utter horror, although the TV screen had been blown out, the image of Edwin still remained there in the smoke that remained.

He was still talking at me.

"You will not have your way Edgar."

"Just you wait!" I cried back at him.

Tolstoy sheltered Ruth and Bobby under his arms as the wretched creatures snivelled.

"This is too scary kids – let's forget about the whole thing."

"What! You can't!" I cried. "I will have my revenge!

"You'll see nothing published by us!" said Tolstoy with a commanding tone.

Enraged by his comment I went up to him and punched him square on the nose. He staggered backward still holding the kids under his arms.

"Right! That's it. I never want to see or hear from you ever again Hyde," he shouted.

The next moment two security guards burst into the room.

"That's the madman!" cried Tolstoy as he pointed at me. "Throw him out!"

The guards made a grab for me, but unable to get a firm grip on my wriggling body, I escaped out of the office door. I sprinted down a corridor and found a sign pointing to a fire escape. With the guards in hot pursuit I hurtled down seventeen flights of stairs and out into the reception area on the ground floor. Another guard at the entrance approached me but I bundled him out of the way.

In a state of blind panic and rage I flew across a busy road with several cars having to screech to a halt to avoid crashing into me. They beeped their horns and shook their fists at me, but my mind was now in a whirl over the thought that Edwin was about to thwart me again.

Then I looked up at a huge billboard and froze. It was where a giant poster should have been to advertise my books. I felt my spirit weaken as I gazed at the image. There stood a giant picture of Edwin with his finger pointing at me. The caption read:

"Edgar you shall not have your way!"

I clenched my fists in anger and began to stagger along the street. How could it all go wrong so quickly? What could I do now?

Coming upon a row of shops I saw myself in the windows. I could see my body was starting to shrink and fade away. No, it mustn't be! Edwin's spell must be taking effect again. I was being drawn back into the spirit world.

Feeling weaker and weaker I found myself standing at a book shop. There, in the window, was a display where my books should have been. I knew my fun was over when I looked at the cover of each and every one of the books. They all had the same picture on the front of them. Edwin the sorcerer!

I knew the end was near again as I looked at my reflection in the window. My body was fading away with every second that passed. Suddenly, another reflection appeared in the window. It was old Edwin.

"I must send you back to the spirit world," he said. "These children have done you no wrong."

It was only then that I realised that I had brought about my own downfall. I had chosen Ruth and Bobby to help me because their heads were full of dark and evil thoughts. As I had put so much trust in them, they began to like me too much. Their minds began to fill with good thoughts towards me and Edwin had the chance to recast his spell upon me. Kids! Why are they so unreliable?

With that, I exhaled my last breath and faded away completely.

Chapter 12

Once more I was in the land of the dead!

In an instant I was back in the empty void where I had only, so recently, escaped from. Once more I was to roam the endless nothingness in which Edwin had imprisoned me. It's just not fair!

I could not feel the ground under my feet or the air in my lungs. The sun did not warm my skin or the winds ruffle my hair. There was no thirst or hunger. I was once again deprived of all the pleasures and sensations of being alive.

Through the long and torturous centuries, I had awaited my chance to be free again, and just when I thought revenge was mine, out popped old Edwin again. The old fool's sense of timing was deplorable.

How did he know what was happening? He must have sensed that I had broken his spell and was about to have my revenge. Maybe Edwin had been watching over me all along?

Then I became aware of the presence of another spirit in my realm. It was a feeling that made my soul shiver. It could only be the spirit of the man who had imprisoned my soul again.

It was Edwin!

"What are you doing here?" I cried. "Haven't you caused me enough trouble?"

"For a learned man, Edgar, you are sometimes very foolish," Edwin replied.

Chapter 12

Enraged by his insult I screamed, "How dare you? What do you mean?"

"Edgar, I'm a sorcerer. I can travel between the living and the dead. I have the knowledge. It's what sorcerers do you fool!" he replied.

"You mean you've been keeping an eye on me all along?" I questioned him.

"I've popped in to keep an eye on you every now and then," the sorcerer said.

Confused I asked, "Then why have I never felt your presence in the spirit world before?"

Edwin shook his head at my question as if saddened by my lack of understanding.

"I'm a sorcerer. I have mystical powers that you will never understand, Edgar. You like to think that you are intelligent and better than everyone else is, but you are really only a tutor from the 15th century," he said.

I was outraged at this explanation and stated, "That's not fair!"

Edwin shook his head.

"Fairness has nothing to do with it. I must protect all the children."

"I'll find a way to sort you," I said menacingly.

Edwin smiled in a smug way.

"You'll have a long time to work on that idea. Goodbye, Edgar, I must be moving along now," he said.

Angry that his presence was going to depart so quickly when I had so many questions for him, I snapped at him.

"Why are you leaving?"

The sorcerer sighed.

"Edgar, you are not the centre of the universe. I have other matters to deal with that are more important than watching over you."

His answer really annoyed me. Who could be more important than me?

Chapter 12

With these final words he was gone again. I was totally alone in my soul prison once again.

So, now I was back again in limbo with nowhere to go and nothing to do. Spirits like mine just float around the earth without feeling or sensing anything that a living person would. Tragic, is the only word to describe what's happened to me.

Time passed slowly, once again, as my spirit roamed the emptiness. I had to plan another scheme to escape my soul prison.

Edwin, the sorcerer, would rue the day when he dared to interfere in my business. He might have me on the run at the moment, but I would return again. My soul ached for revenge upon him and the children of the earth. How I loathed them.

Then it came to me in a blinding flash. I would have to tell my terrible tales from beyond the grave. Using people, such as my devoted Hugo, I could get my devilish tales into print. Then, as children's heads filled with the evil stories I would stand a chance of coming back from the dead again.

There was always the chance that Edwin would turn up and spoil things for me, but that was a chance I would have to take. He had said that I was not very important, so maybe I could escape my soul prison while he was busy doing something else. I even dreamed that he would by crushed by a powerful enemy and the spell on me would be broken.

Ah, such dreams. If only they would become real.

Until then I'll keep plugging away with my naughty little stories to fill your minds with nasty thoughts instead of good ones.

Thank you for reading this book. I hope you enjoyed my tale and will take the time to read some more of my works.

Chapter 12

You have helped me in my quest to come back again. One day I shall be back in the land of the living. Edwin will be defeated by my power and I shall have my revenge on all you children out there.

Watch out!

We hope you enjoyed this story from the pen of Edgar J. Hyde. Here are some other titles in the Creepers series for you to collect:

The Ghostly Soldier

Doctor Death

Happy Halloween

Soul Harvest

Blood on Tap

Mirror Mirror

The Piano

The Scarecrow

This series was conceived by Edgar J Hyde and much of the text was provided by his minions under slavish conditions and pain of death! Thankfully none of the minions defied their master and so we can say 'thank you' to them for toughing it out and making this series possible

Doctor Death

Have you ever gone to the doctor with a minor illness only to find that you feel even worse? That's what happens to Josh Stevens and his friends. They turn from a bunch of healthy kids into smelly, greasy, pustulent wrecks – and coincidentally they have all just paid a visit to the charming and handsome Doctor Blair. Josh's hideous boils are jeopardising a future date with the lovely Karen but there are much more sinister "remedies" lurking in the good doctor's medicine cupboard. But how can Josh and his friends stop Doctor Death carrying out his deadly plan?

The Ghostly Soldier

Angus and Ishbel love to hear the stories about heroic Scottish warriors. They visit the site where the Battle of Culloden was fought and Angus romanticises the events, wishing that he could have been there to help fight the Redcoats. His opinion changes when an explosion in their garden unleashes the spirits of ghostly warriors from the battle. Angus is accidentally caught up in the terrifying world of the restless spirits of English and Scottish soldiers who must fight the battle again and again. The children must return the spirits to where they belong, but how?

Soul Harvest

The Grimaldis, a creepy new family who have a bad attitude and who dress entirely in black move into Billy and Alice's neighbourhood. Very soon afterwards their mum and dad and all the other neighbours start to act very strangely – as if they have suddenly become wicked. The children, and their friends Ricky and Alex, are soon the only normal ones left in a neighbourhood of thieves, bullies and thugs. The entire village, headed by the Grimaldis, are soon trying to find the four children and capture their souls to make the imminent "harvest" complete!

𝔅lood on 𝔗ap

Bill Todd is delighted to have found a new house for his family. It's cheap, in a good neighbourhood and it will provide the much-needed space for his growing family. His wife and his young children – Alex Beth, Gary and Karen – are not so sure. The house looks sinister and feels even more creepy. They all have a very bad feeling about it, but Mr Todd will not change his mind. Number 13 Blackday Avenue is *just* what it appears to be, and very soon they encounter something that makes them wish they had never moved!

Ghost Writer

Charlie is a 15-year-old, budding writer. When his family move to a large old house in the country he becomes the unsuspecting contact for a spirit writer who is trying to communicate with the living. How can the strange passages that appear overnight, in Charlie's own handwriting, be the work of anyone else but him? Who will believe his incredible story? The ghost seems to be trying to tell him of a dark secret and a cruel injustice. When Charlie starts to have a chilling recurring dream about his own death and he and his brother, Neil and sister, Kate start to see apparitions, they decide that they must investigate the ghost writer's secret - with terrifying consequences!

Mirror Mirror

When she and her family visit a local antique shop to buy a fabulous mirror, Sophie is tranfixed by a music box ballerina and insists that she must have it. Little do any of the family know of the dark and tragic history behind the mirror and the music box, and their link to the person who calls herself the Keeper of Lost Souls. Sophie and her sisters, Amy-Beth and Lucy , with the help of their unpredictable Aunty Patsy, must discover the true story of the girl in the mirror. They must free her from the terrifying past that the mirror has witnessed and makes her relive again and again.

The Piano

Roger and Emily Houston can't believe the bargain they have found when they buy a piano for a mere £200 - just perfect for the piano lessons of their children Victoria and Darryn. Their delight soon turns to amazement and horror - the piano has a life (or is that a death?) of it's own. The melodies that it plays over and over again are (literally) haunting and it becomes clear that someone from their past has a message for the Houston family about a very important decision they are about to make.

The Scarecrow

A horrific attack takes place on an isolated farm. A shivering, terrified man is found in shock, his tongue removed. The shock is too much for him and he kills himself leaving a note which claims that he was a burglar who was stopped from breaking into the farm by a scarecrow, who then ripped out his tongue. Of course no-one believes the note. But, David, who lives on the farm, knows that the noisy farmyard cockerel has been found throttled, his beloved dog has mysteriously gone missing and Jonesy a harmless local character has also been viciously silenced - they must be connected with the sightings of a scruffy, barely-human creature on the prowl. David decides he must solve the mystery himself but doesn't realise just what he is getting himself into.